HAPPILY EVER AFTER

Wicked Stepmothers

KATE RIGGS

CREATIVE EDUCATION

COPYRIGHT

Published by Creative Education
P.O. Box 227, Mankato, Minnesota 56002
Creative Education is an imprint of
The Creative Company
www.thecreativecompany.us

Design by Stephanie Blumenthal
Production by Christine Vanderbeek
Art direction by Rita Marshall
Printed in the United States of America

Photographs by Alamy (AF archive, Moviestore Collection Ltd, Pictorial Press Ltd), Dover Publications Inc. (Children's Book Illustrations; Imps, Elves, Fairies & Goblins), Graphic Frames (Agile Rabbit Editions), iStockphoto (Geoffrey Holman, Jens Carsten Rosemann, Duncan Walker), Mary Evans Picture Library (Mary Evans Picture Library, Peter & Dawn Cope Collection), Shutterstock (Denis Barbulat, Giant Stock, Sergej Razvodovskij)

Illustration page 17 © 2001 Etienne Delessert

Library of Congress Cataloging-in-Publication Data
Riggs, Kate.
Wicked stepmothers / by Kate Riggs.
p. cm. — (Happily ever after)
Summary: A primer of the familiar fairy-tale characters of wicked stepmothers, from what makes them scary to those they harm, plus famous stories and movies in which they have appeared.
Includes index.
ISBN 978-1-60818-245-9
1. Fairy tales. 2. Stepmothers in literature. 3. Stepmothers—Juvenile literature. I. Title.

GR550.R456 2013
398.2—dc23   2011051177

First edition
9 8 7 6 5 4 3 2 1

TABLE OF CONTENTS

The Beginning **4**

Marrying into the Family **6**

Scary Lady **8**

Evil Plotting **10**

Killing Time **12**

Tricks and Tips **14**

The Fairest of Them All **16**

Love Is Best **19**

The End **20**

Write Your Own Fairy Tale **22**

Glossary **23**

Read More **23**

Web Sites **24**

Index **24**

*"Once upon a time, there was a **wicked** stepmother. She was jealous of her beautiful stepdaughter."*

Wicked stepmothers are characters you can find in fairy tales. A fairy tale is a story about magical people and places.

Wicked stepmothers marry fairy tale kings. Sometimes they marry other rich men who are not kings. Wicked stepmothers are not nice people. They are mean to anyone they don't like.

A wicked stepmother may be pretty. But she is mostly scary. Some wicked stepmothers use magic to cast spells. They **compete** with their stepchildren for love and power.

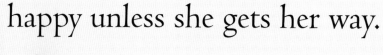

The wicked stepmother plays the part of the **villain**. She is not a likeable character. She thinks of evil things to do. The wicked stepmother is not happy unless she gets her way.

A wicked stepmother tries to get rid of her beautiful stepdaughter. She may want the stepdaughter to go away. Or she may want the stepdaughter to die! The stepdaughter is often a princess.

A princess needs help to beat her wicked stepmother. A fairy godmother or a prince helps a princess. Sometimes they use magic. Other times they trick the wicked stepmother.

Snow *White* is a story about a beautiful princess with a jealous stepmother. The queen tries to kill Snow White. When Snow White eats a **poisoned** apple, she falls asleep. She later wakes up and marries a prince. The wicked stepmother dies.

The Disney movie *Cinderella* is about
a girl with a wicked stepmother named
Lady Tremaine. Lady Tremaine has
two daughters she loves. But she treats
Cinderella badly. Yet Cinderella marries
a prince and escapes
her wicked
stepmother.

THE END

Wicked stepmothers do not have happy endings. Everyone else does, though!

"The princess woke up from a deep sleep. She married her prince. The wicked stepmother disappeared. And everyone else lived happily ever after."

Copy this short story onto a sheet of paper.
Then fill in the blanks with your own words!

Once upon a time, a wicked woman named _____

married a king. They lived in a castle called _____. The king

had a beautiful daughter. Her name was _____. The wicked

stepmother did not like _____. She tried to _____ her.

_____ helped the princess _____. The wicked

stepmother was very _____! She _____.

The princess married _____. They lived happily

ever after.

GLOSSARY

compete—try to be or do something better than someone else

jealous—wanting what someone else has; wanting to be like someone else

poisoned—treated with poison, or something that can hurt or kill a person

villain—a character who does evil things

wicked—bad or evil

READ MORE

Skinner, Daphne. *My Side of the Story: by Cinderella / My Side of the Story: by Lady Tremaine.* New York: Disney Press, 2003.

———. *My Side of the Story: by Snow White / My Side of the Story: by the Queen.* New York: Disney Press, 2003.

WEB SITES

Cinderella Games
http://www.funnygames.co.uk/cinderella-games.html
Help Cinderella escape her wicked stepmother and get to the ball!

Snow White Coloring Pages and Activities
http://disney.go.com/disneyjunior/princess/princess-snow-white-coloring-create
Download pictures to color, and make a puppet of the evil queen!

INDEX

Cinderella 19

fairy godmothers 14

fairy tales 4, 6

kings 6

Lady Tremaine 19

magic 4, 8, 14

poisoned apples 16

princes 14, 16, 19, 20

princesses 12, 14, 16, 20

Snow White 16

spells 8

wicked stepmother
characteristics 4, 6, 8,
10, 12